WINNING ELECTIONS

YOU TOO CAN BECOME PEOPLE'S REPRESENTATIVE !

LOGESH ARUMUGAM & GIRI K S

Made with ♥ on the Notion Press Platform
www.notionpress.com

With gratitude to the Universe, for being the inspiration behind every discovery and creation.

Contents

Contents

Preface

Winning Elections is an easy-to-follow resource designed for aspiring candidates and political enthusiasts in India. This book provides comprehensive insights into the electoral process and equips readers with practical tools and strategies to prepare for and win elections. Featuring simple checklists and templates, it simplifies the journey from candidacy to victory, making it accessible for everyone.

Section 1: Understanding Elections in India

CHAPTER ONE

Introduction

The **First section** of the book covers a range of topics related to the various types of elections in India, including Lok Sabha, Rajya Sabha, Legislative Assembly, and local body elections. It also delves into the roles and responsibilities of elected representatives, providing a clear understanding of what is expected from those who hold public office. Through detailed explanations and real-life examples, readers will gain a solid foundation of the electoral landscape and the duties that come with being a people's representative.

The **Second section** provides checklists and templates for pre-campaign preparations before the election. It includes:

- **Self Discovery 360 Degree Feedback Template:** A tool to gather feedback from peers, mentors, and constituents to understand strengths and areas for improvement.

- **SWOT Analysis Template for Self Analysis and Decision Making:** A structured approach to assess personal strengths, weaknesses, opportunities, and threats.

- **Survey & Research Questionnaire:** Guidance on selecting the right constituency to contest through thorough surveys and research.

- **Setting Campaign Goals:** Methods to define clear and achievable campaign objectives.

- **Connecting with People:** Effective ways to engage with and understand the electorate.

- **Understanding SDGs:** An overview of Sustainable Development Goals and their relevance in campaigning.

- **Campaign Starter and Budget Plan Kit:** Practical tools for organizing and budgeting campaign activities.

With this comprehensive guide, readers will be well-equipped to navigate the complexities of the Indian electoral system and increase their chances of electoral success.

Section Three of **"Winning Elections: A Practical Guide"** outlines essential strategies for effectively engaging with people during election campaigns. This section provides practical insights and actionable advice, this section equips readers with the knowledge and tools needed to connect with voters and run successful election campaigns.

- **Election Process Overview:** A comprehensive guide to understanding the electoral process in India, from nomination to result declaration.

- **Mandatory Compliance:** Detailed explanations of legal and regulatory requirements candidates must adhere to during their campaigns.

- **Approvals and Permissions:** Guidance on obtaining necessary permissions and approvals for campaign activities, ensuring compliance with local laws and regulations.

- **Air Campaign and Ground Campaign Methods:** Strategies for utilizing both traditional media (such as television and radio) and grassroots methods (such as rallies and door-to-door canvassing) to reach voters effectively.

- **Targeting Voters:** Techniques for identifying and targeting key demographic groups and swing voters, maximizing campaign impact.

- **Campaign Impact Chart:** Tools and templates for tracking and analyzing campaign performance and voter engagement metrics.

- **Fitness:** Tips on maintaining physical and mental fitness throughout the demanding election campaign period.

CHAPTER TWO

Various Types of Elections in India

In India, there are several types of elections conducted at different levels of government to elect representatives. Here are the main types of elections:

In India, there are several types of elections conducted at different levels of government to elect representatives. Here are the main types of elections:

1. <u>**Lok Sabha Elections:**</u>

   - Lok Sabha elections are conducted to elect members of the lower house of Parliament, known as the Lok Sabha or House of the People.
   - Members of the Lok Sabha represent constituencies across India based on population.
   -

2. <u>**Rajya Sabha Elections:**</u>

   - Rajya Sabha elections are held to elect members of the upper house of Parliament, known as the Rajya

Sabha or Council of States.

- Members of the Rajya Sabha are not directly elected by the public but are elected by the elected members of State Legislative Assemblies using a single transferable vote system.

-

3. <u>State Legislative Assembly Elections:</u>

- State Legislative Assembly elections are conducted to elect members of the legislative assemblies in the states and union territories of India.
- Members of the legislative assembly (MLAs) represent constituencies within each state or union territory.

-

4. <u>Local Body Elections:</u>

- Local body elections are held to elect representatives to local governing bodies such as municipal corporations, municipal councils, and panchayats (village councils).
- These elections are crucial for local governance and decision-making on issues like infrastructure, sanitation, and local development.

-

5. <u>Panchayat Elections:</u>

- Panchayat elections are specifically for rural local governance bodies, including gram panchayats

(village councils), block panchayats, and district panchayats.
- These elections empower rural communities to manage local affairs and implement development programs.
-

6. <u>Mayor and Corporation Elections:</u>

- In metropolitan areas and large cities, elections are held to elect mayors and municipal corporation members.
- These elections determine local administration and policymaking for urban areas.
-

7. <u>By-elections (or Special Elections):</u>

- By-elections are conducted to fill vacancies that occur between regular elections due to death, resignation, or disqualification of elected representatives.
- These elections ensure continuity in representation and governance.
-

Each type of election plays a crucial role in India's democratic process, allowing citizens to participate in governance at various levels and elect representatives who can address their needs and concerns effectively.

CHAPTER THREE

Elections to President of India & Vice President of India

The president is indirectly elected by an electoral college comprising both houses of the Parliament of India and the legislative assemblies of each of India's states and territories, who themselves are all directly elected by the citizens.

- The president of India is the head of state of the Republic of India.

- The president is the nominal head of the executive, the first citizen of the country.

- President is the commander-in-chief of the Indian Armed Forces.

The vice president is elected indirectly by members of an electoral college consisting of the members of both Houses of Parliament and not the members of state legislative assembly by the system of proportional representation using single transferable votes and the voting is conducted by Election Commission of India via secret ballot.

- The vice president of India is the deputy to the head of state of the Republic of India, i.e. the president of India.

- The office of vice president is the second-highest constitutional office after the president and ranks second in the order of precedence and first in the line of succession to the presidency.

- The vice president is also a member of the Parliament of India as the ex officio chairman of the Rajya Sabha.

CHAPTER FOUR

Elections to Lok Sabha & Rajya Sabha

The **Lok Sabha**, constitutionally the House of the People, is the lower house of India's bicameral Parliament, with the upper house being the Rajya Sabha. Members of the Lok Sabha are elected by an adult universal suffrage and a first-past-the-post system to represent their respective constituencies, and they hold their seats for five years or until the body is dissolved by the President on the advice of the council of ministers.

- The maximum size of the Lok Sabha as outlined in the Constitution of India is 552 members, made up of up to 524 members representing the people of 28 states and 19 members representing people of 8 Union territories based on their population

- A total of 131 seats (24.03%) are reserved for representatives of Scheduled Castes (84) and Scheduled Tribes (47).

The **Rajya Sabha**, constitutionally the Council of States, is the upper house of the bicameral Parliament of India.

- As of 2022, it has a maximum membership of 245, of which 233 are elected by the legislatures of the states and union territories using single transferable votes through open ballots, while the president can appoint 12 members for their contributions to art, literature, science, and social services.

State/ UT* & Seats:

- Andaman and Nicobar Islands* - 1
- Andhra Pradesh - 25
- Arunachal Pradesh - 2
- Assam - 14
- Bihar - 40
- Chandigarh* - 1
- Chhattisgarh - 11
- DNH & DD* - 2
- Delhi (NCT)* - 7
- Goa - 2
- Gujarat - 26
- Haryana - 10
- Himachal Pradesh - 4
- Jammu and Kashmir* - 5
- Jharkhand - 14
- Karnataka - 28
- Kerala- 20
- Ladakh* - 1
- Lakshadweep* - 1
- Madhya Pradesh - 29
- Maharashtra - 48
- Manipur - 2
- Meghalaya - 2
- Mizoram - 1

- Nagaland - 1
- Odisha - 21
- Puducherry* - 1
- Punjab - 13
- Rajasthan - 25
- Sikkim - 1
- Tamil Nadu - 39
- Telangana - 17
- Tripura - 2
- Uttarakhand - 5
- Uttar Pradesh - 80
- West Bengal - 42
- **Total: 543**

CHAPTER FIVE

State Legislative Assembly & State Legislative Council

The **State Legislative Assembly**, or Vidhan Sabha, or also Saasana Sabha, is a legislative body in the states and union territories of India. In the 28 states and 3 union territories with a unicameral state legislature, it is the sole legislative body and in 6 states it is the lower house of their bicameral state legislatures with the upper house being State Legislative Council. 5 union territories are governed directly by the Union Government of India and have no legislative body.

Statewise - No of Assembly Seats: Assembly, Capital, House Strength

- Andhra Pradesh, Amaravati, 175
- Arunachal Pradesh, Itanagar, 60
- Assam, Dispur, 126
- Bihar, Patna, 243
- Chhattisgarh, Raipur, 90
- Delhi, New Delhi, 70

- Goa, Panaji, 40
- Gujarat, Gandhinagar, 182
- Haryana, Chandigarh, 90
- Himachal Pradesh, Shimla (summer), Dharamshala (winter), 68
- Jammu and Kashmir, Srinagar (summer), Jammu (Winter), 90
- Jharkhand, Ranchi, 81
- Karnataka Bangalore, 224
- Kerala, Thiruvananthapuram, 140
- Madhya Pradesh, Bhopal, 230
- Maharashtra, Mumbai, 288
- Manipur, Imphal, 60
- Meghalaya, Shillong, 60
- Mizoram, Aizawl, 40
- Nagaland, Kohima, 60
- Odisha, Bhubaneshwar, 147
- Puducherry, Puducherry, 33
- Punjab, Chandigarh, 117
- Rajasthan,Jaipur, 200
- Sikkim, Gangtok, 32
- Tamil Nadu, Chennai, 234
- Telangana, Hyderabad, 119
- Tripura, Agartala, 60
- Uttar Pradesh, Lucknow, 403
- Uttarakhand Bhararisain (summer), Dehradun (Winter), 70
- West Bengal, Kolkata,294

Total — 4123

The **State Legislative Council**, or Vidhan Parishad, or Saasana Mandali is the upper house in those states of India that have a bicameral state legislature; the lower house being the State Legislative Assembly. Its establishment is defined in Article 169 of the Constitution of India. As of 2022, 6 out of 28 states have a State Legislative Council. These are Andhra Pradesh, Karnataka, Telangana, Maharashtra, Bihar, and Uttar Pradesh.

CHAPTER SIX

Elections to Local Governance Bodies

The local governance entities are broadly classified into urban and rural, which are further sub-divided based on the size of population in case of the urban bodies and based on the size of population and hierarchy in case of the rural bodies.

<u>Urban local governance bodies:</u>The following 3 types of democratically elected urban local governance bodies in India are called municipalities and abbreviated as the "MC". These are classified based on the size of the population of the urban settlement.

- Municipal Corporation, also called the "Nagar Nigam", of cities with more than 1 million populations.

- Municipal Councils, also called the "Nagar Palika", of cities with more than 25,000 and less than 1 million populations.

- Municipal Committee, also called the "Town Council" or "Nagar Panchayat" or "Town Panchayat" or "Notified Area Council" depending on the state within which they lie, these are in the town with more than 10,000 and less than 25,000 population.

<u>Rural local governance bodies</u>: The democratically elected local governance bodies in the villages of rural India are called Panchayati Raj Institutions (PRIs) which are based on the vedic era native democratic panchayat (Council of five officials) system. The following 3 hierarchies of PRI panchayats exist in states or Union Territories with more than two million inhabitants:

- Gram Panchayats at village level
- Panchayat Samiti/Mandal Parishad at Community Development Block/Mandal level
- Zila Parishad at district level.

Elections to Local Bodies in every state are conducted once in five years to elect the representatives to the Urban and Rural local bodies. These elections are conducted by respective State Election Commission.. Both direct and indirect elections apply for local bodies. Direct election posts include:

- **Urban bodies**

  ◦ Corporation Mayor
  ◦ Municipality/Town Panchayat Chairperson
  ◦ Corporation/Municipality/Town Panchayat Councillor
  ◦

- **Rural bodies**

  - Village Panchayat President
  - District Panchayat councillor
  - Panchayat Union councillor
  - Village Panchayat Ward Member

Village panchayats (Tamil: ஊராட்சிகள்) form the grass-root level of democracy as they form the local government for the basic building blocks of India - villages. Village panchayat president himself/herself is an executive authority here.

Panchayat Unions (coterminous with blocks) (Tamil: ஊராட்சி ஒன்றியம்) is the group of Village panchayats. They serve as the link between the villages and the district administration. They form the local government at the Taluk level. Panchayat Union council consists of elected ward members from the villages. It is headed by a panchayat union chairperson, who is elected indirectly by the ward members of the council.

District panchayats in state (Tamil: மாவட்ட ஊராட்சி ஒன்றியங்கள்) form the cream of the panchayat raj system. They take the top slot with mainly advisory powers to the rest. Developmental administration of the district in rural areas are in its hands. It consists of ward members elected from various villages in its jurisdiction. It is presided by a district panchayat chairperson, who is indirectly elected by its ward members.. District collector is the ex-officio chairman of the District rural development agency.

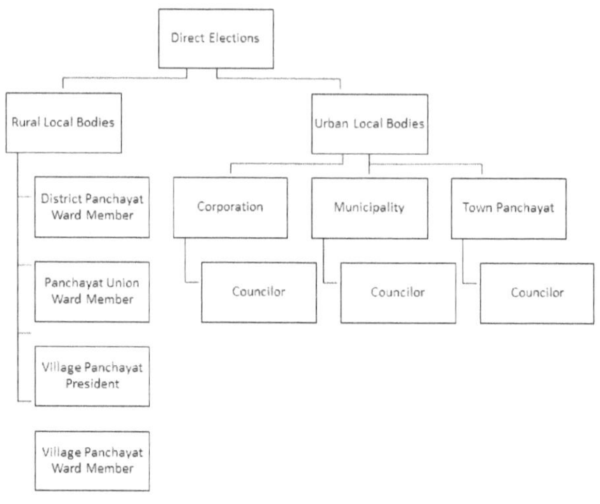

Direct Elections

Indirect election posts include Chairpersons of District panchayats and Panchayat unions, Deputy Mayor of corporations, Vice-Chairpersons of Municipalities and Town panchayats. Various statutory/standing committees are also elected by the way of indirect elections.

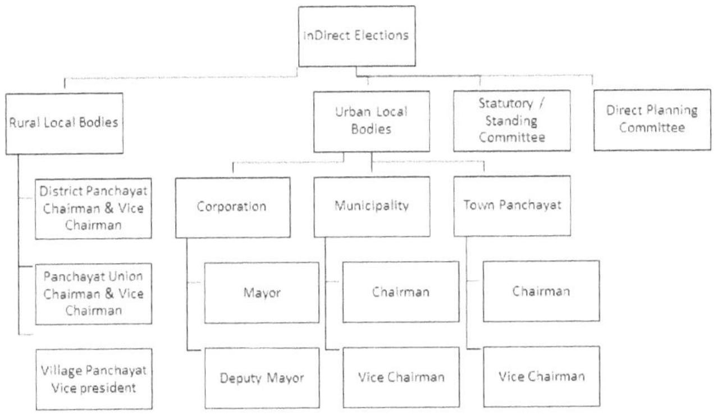

Indirect Elections

Roles and responsibilities of elected representative

<u>Some of the qualifications to become people representative are ..</u>

- The person must be a citizen of India
- The person must have completed the age of 25 years
- The person must not hold an office of profit
- The person must possess qualifications laid down by the Parliament of India
- The person must not be of unsound mind and should not have been disqualified by a competent court
- The person should not be convicted of any offence and sentenced to an imprisonment of 2 years or more.

<u>Roles and Responsibilities of an MP:</u>

- Legislative responsibility: To pass Laws of India in the Lok Sabha.
- Oversight responsibility: To ensure that the executive (i.e. government) performs its duties satisfactorily.
- Representative responsibility: To represent the views and aspirations of the people of their constituency in the Parliament of India (Lok Sabha).
- Power of the purse responsibility: To approve and oversee the revenues and expenditures proposed by the government.
- The Union Council of Ministers, who are also members of parliament have an additional responsibility of the executive as compared to those who are not in the Council of Ministers

Roles and Responsibilities of an MLA:

A Member of the Legislative Assembly (MLA) is a representative elected by the voters of an electoral district (constituency) to the legislature of State government in the Indian system of government. From each constituency, the people elect one representative who then becomes a member of the Legislative Assembly (MLA). The most important function of the legislature is law making. The state legislature has the power to make laws on all items on which Parliament cannot legislate. Some of these items are police, prisons, irrigation, agriculture, local governments, public health, Pilgrimage, and burial grounds.

Roles and Responsibilities of a Local Body Representative:

They are responsible for the implementation of various centrally sponsored, state-funded, and externally aided schemes for provision of basic amenities and other services to the people. Local authorities are multi-purpose bodies responsible for delivering a broad range of services in relation to roads; traffic; planning; housing; economic and community development; environment, recreation and amenity services; fire services and maintaining the register of electors.

Section 2 : Interest & Awareness: Preparation Before the Election / Pre- Campaign

CHAPTER EIGHT

Self Evaluation : Are you a Leader ?

Leadership Skill, Self discovery 360 degree feedback:

Before deciding to contest and become an elected representative, it is essential to undertake a thorough self-evaluation to assess whether you possess the leadership skills necessary to lead effectively from the front. Rate yourself for the below parameters in the scale of 1- 3 (1 : High, 2: Medium, 3: Low) and also ask your family members & friends also to rate you on the below parameters and see where do you stand and decide whether you can be an leader. More the rating is High for the parameters then you can decide to contest the elections and lead from front.

- **Vision : Power of seeing the future**
- Your Rating:
- Your Family Members Rating about you:
- Your Friends Rating Rating about you:

- **Courage : Mental strength, Withstand difficulty**

- Your Rating:

- Your Family Members Rating about you:
- Your Friends Rating Rating about you:

- <u>**Integrity : Quality of being honest**</u>

- Your Rating:
- Your Family Members Rating about you:
- Your Friends Rating Rating about you:

- <u>**Humility : Quality of being humble (respectful / Modest)**</u>

- Your Rating:
- Your Family Members Rating about you:
- Your Friends Rating Rating about you:

- <u>**Strategic planning: Create, Implement & evaluating the results of executing the plan**</u>
- Your Rating:
- Your Family Members Rating about you:
- Your Friends Rating Rating about you:

- <u>**Focus : Paying Attention (Interest)**</u>
- Your Rating:
- Your Family Members Rating about you:
- Your Friends Rating Rating about you:

- <u>**Collaborative : Working together with somebody else to achieve some common goal**</u>
- Your Rating:
- Your Family Members Rating about you:
- Your Friends Rating Rating about you:

- <u>**Positive Attitude: Paying attention to the good, rather than bad in people, situations, events.**</u>

- Your Rating:
- Your Family Members Rating about you:
- Your Friends Rating Rating about you:

- <u>**Social Connect : Network with People, Business and society**</u>

- Your Rating:
- Your Family Members Rating about you:
- Your Friends Rating Rating about you:

- <u>**Solution Mindset: Providing logical solutions to problems / issues**</u>

- Your Rating:
- Your Family Members Rating about you:
- Your Friends Rating Rating about you:

<u>**SWOT Analysis for Self-Evaluation & Decision Making:**</u>

SWOT analysis is indeed a valuable strategic planning tool used across various domains, including personal development and decision-making processes. It helps individuals assess their internal strengths and weaknesses, as well as external opportunities and threats. This structured approach enables a thorough evaluation of factors that can influence one's ability to achieve goals or make informed decisions. In the context of preparing to contest and become an elected representative, conducting a

SWOT analysis can be highly beneficial. Here's how it can be applied:

SWOT Analysis for Self-Evaluation:

Strengths:

- Identify personal qualities, skills, and experiences that make you a strong candidate.
- Highlight leadership abilities, communication skills, knowledge of local issues, etc.

Weaknesses:

- Acknowledge areas where improvement is needed or where you may face challenges.
- Consider aspects such as lack of experience in certain areas, communication barriers, or organizational skills.

Opportunities:

- Explore external factors that could benefit your campaign or role as a representative.
- Look at trends in voter preferences, support from community leaders, or emerging issues that align with your platform.

Threats:

- Identify external challenges or obstacles that could affect your candidacy or effectiveness as a representative.
- Consider factors like strong competition from other candidates, negative public perception, or external political dynamics.

My Strength	My Weakness
My Opportunities	My Threat

Self Evaluation - SWOT

By leveraging SWOT analysis as a tool for self-evaluation, aspiring candidates can better understand their readiness to contest elections, strategically plan their campaigns, and enhance their effectiveness as elected representatives.

CHAPTER NINE

How to Select the right constituency to contest

Selecting the right constituency to contest in an election is a crucial decision that can significantly impact your chances of success as a candidate. Here's a structured approach to help you select the right constituency:

- Which is the constituency you are planning to contest ?

- What is the total population in the constituency ?

- Research & Understand about the existing political landscape in the area where you would like to contest ?

- Research & Understand the social landscape (Religion, Caste) of the area where you would like to contest ?

- What is the Type of election you are planning to contest ?

- Find out the Rules and also check whether you are eligible to contest

- Find out the characteristics of the constituency / area where you are planning to contest. – Whether it is Urban / Rural / Semi Rural ?

- What are the various characteristics of the voters ? – How many Male Voters / How Many female voters / How many Third Gender / Age wise voters

- Find out what has happened in the previous election ? Winners, Losers, Margins, local Issues – Solved / Un Solved list ?

- Who could be your possible opponents?

- Strength and Weakness of Opponents?

- How many people (not just voters) live in your district?

- What percentage of these voters do you expect to vote in this election?

- How many candidates will be running for this position?

- How many of these candidates could be considered serious opponents ?

- What percentage of the votes cast will be needed to win?

- On average, how many voters live in one household?

- How many households will you need to communicate with for your message to reach enough voters to achieve victory?

Selecting the right constituency involves a combination of strategic analysis, personal connection, and practical considerations. By carefully evaluating these factors, you can enhance your candidacy's prospects and effectively represent the interests of the constituents you seek to serve.

Setting a campaign goal: Is it possible for me ?

- In a multi candidate election, the winning candidate received 30% of the vote or 15,000 votes.
- If you convert the votes in to houses, this would come to 7500 houses, assuming an average of two votes from every household.
- You cannot assume that every voter will you talk will vote for you
- You should have a plan to reach out to more than 20,000 voters or 10,000 houses.
- Suppose if you convince 5 out of 10 voters you talk, you will need to talk to 40,000 voters or 20,000 houses.
- Narrow the group of people you need to convince and have a clear reach out plan to cover the entire region of the constituency

CHAPTER TEN

Connecting with People

Building meaningful connections with people should start well before the announcement of elections. Here's how you can begin connecting with potential voters effectively, focusing on relevant talk points:

<u>1. Identify Relevant Issues:</u>

- **Local Concerns:** Research and understand the specific issues and concerns that matter most to people in your target constituency.

- **Community Feedback:** Listen to the voices of local residents through community meetings, surveys, and informal conversations.

<u>2. Develop Talk Points:</u>

- **Clear Messaging:** Craft clear and concise messages that resonate with voters' concerns and aspirations.

- **Solution-Oriented:** Focus on offering solutions and actionable plans to address identified issues.

3. Engage Proactively:

- **Community Events:** Attend local events, social gatherings, and festivals to meet people and build connections.

- **Door-to-Door Campaigning:** Initiate door-to-door canvassing to introduce yourself, listen to concerns, and discuss your platform.

4. Utilize Technology:

- **Social Media:** Use social media platforms to share updates, engage in discussions, and reach a broader audience.

- **Online Forums:** Participate in local online forums, groups, and community pages to interact with residents virtually.

5. Build Relationships:

- **Personal Touch:** Show genuine interest in people's lives and issues. Build trust through active listening and empathy.

- **Accessibility:** Make yourself accessible by responding promptly to inquiries, emails, and messages from constituents.

6. Educate and Inform:

- **Policy Discussions:** Organize town hall meetings or discussion forums to educate voters about key policies and initiatives.

- **Information Dissemination:** Distribute informative pamphlets, newsletters, or digital content outlining your vision and plans.

7. Community Involvement:

- **Volunteer and Support:** Get involved in community service activities and local initiatives to demonstrate your commitment to the constituency.

- **Collaborate:** Partner with local leaders, organizations, and influencers to amplify your outreach efforts.

8. Long-Term Engagement:

- **Consistency:** Maintain regular communication and engagement with constituents beyond election periods.

- **Follow-Up:** Follow up on issues raised by residents and provide updates on actions taken or progress made.

By starting early and focusing on relevant talk points that resonate with people's concerns, you can establish strong connections, build trust, and lay a solid foundation of support well before the election campaign intensifies. This proactive approach not only enhances your visibility but also positions you as a responsive and accountable candidate who genuinely cares about the community's welfare.

What is SDG's ?

The Sustainable Development Goals or Global Goals are a collection of 17 interlinked global goals designed to be a "blueprint to achieve a better and more sustainable future for all". The SDGs were set up in 2015 by the United Nations General Assembly and are intended to be achieved by the year 2030.

Talk points for connecting with people: SDG Goals Vs. Action Plan / Solution Mapping

SDG, [Find out the Current Scenario for each SDG], [Come up with Action Plan or Solution]

1. Poverty
2. Hunger
3. Health & well being
4. Quality Education
5. Gender Equality
6. Clean Water and Sanitation
7. Affordable and Clean Energy
8. Decent Work and Economic growth
9. Industries, Innovation, Infrastructure
10. Reduced Inequality
11. Sustainable Cities and Communities
12. Responsible Consumption and Production
13. Climate Action
14. Climate change and its impact
15. Life below water – Ocean, Sea
16. Life on Land – Forest
17. Peace Justice and Strong Institutions
18. Partnership for growth

<u>Ways to deepen Your Connections With people:</u>

Pay Attention	First Impression	Remember Name	Connect with Story	Groundwork
Spark Interest	Hear Point of Views of Others	Schedule Quality Time	Show Care	

Ways to Connect with People !

- **Pay Attention** : Really focus on what they are saying and pay attention to the details they give.

- **Good First Impression**: Be aware of your expressions, tone of voice and gestures - Smile, Making eye contact

- **Remember Name:** Remembering name of the person and able to address with their name instantly make them feel good

- **Connect with Story**: Use story telling to give a glimpse of who you are and what you believe

- **Groundwork** : Do the groundwork ahead of time, before you reach out to people so that you can answer their questions and help keep your conversation moving

- **Spark Interest** : Make sure you stand out from the crowd in your conversations and put a smile on people's faces

- **Learning with your heart**: Be open to hearing other point of views

- **How you care & Schedule quality time:** Be genuine and show empathy and kindness

- **Remain Unforgettable:** Make sure you are remembered in one's memory for a long time.

- **Provide massive help:** Even the biggest and most powerful people in the world have something they'd like help with. keep helping people.

CHAPTER ELEVEN

Campaign Starter Kit & Budget for the campaign

Campaign Starter Kit

Candidate Profile:

- Engage voters with a brief introduction
- What unique skills and experience have you that will make you the best person for the job?
- What has prepared you for this position?

- ◦ Describe a similar situation where you had success and how you achieved it.
- ◦ Explain any goals you have for transformation?
- ◦ Provide your voters with the steps you are planning to take that will make the changes needed.
- ◦ Add photos of your service to the society

Problems and Solutions of the constituency:

- Problem #1:
- Solution to the problem :

- Problem #2:
- Solution to the problem :

- Problem #3:
- Solution to the problem :

Readiness with Digital Posters, Audio, Video and short messages

- Create catchy digital posters with themes for the campaign: Should cover problem statement and solution you are providing, Create posters of different size in digital format.
- Audio, Video & Short Messages: Create Audio, Video and short messages with the following topics:
- About You

- How are you planning to transform the constituency?
- Solutions you are planning to implement
- Together how you are planning to transform life of people

Make sure the audio / video messages are of less than 60 seconds and the short messages are catchy and to the point.

Team required for election campaign:

Election Campaign Team

- 1 Campaign Manager
- 1 Legal Expert
- 2 Office Manager (who answers phones, handles requests)
- 3 Program managers responsible for hand holding and co-ordination with others
- 1 Finance Manager: Plan Budget and also to keep track of all receivables and expenses
- 1 or 2 Legal experts

- 1 Content Creator responsible for drafting the literature and getting it printed
- 2 Designers: Creating Posters / Banners
- 50-60 temporary staff to connect with people during elections

The above team required for an assembly election. Based on the type of the election the no of team member varies.

Role of Campaign Manager:

Therefore the role of the campaign manager is to run the campaign. This must be someone in which the candidate has complete confidence. After all, this should be the most important thing in both of their lives for the relatively short period of time that the campaign will last. In a sense, the candidate is the heart of the campaign and the campaign manager is the brain. A good campaign needs both to be effective but they have very distinct roles to play.

Too often candidates want to run their own campaign. They either do not choose a campaign manager or choose someone they think they can manipulate. In either case they end up spending too much time making decisions that should be left to someone else, which takes time from their main job, meeting voters and donors.

A campaign manager must make sure the candidate is scheduled to meet voters, they must deal with or otherwise supervise those who will deal with the press, the money, the other methods of voter contact and everything else planned (and unplanned) during the campaign.

Volunteering & Fundraising:

Once you decide to contest you should begin raising the money needed and also get help from your dear ones to support for your campaign. You can create online form...

Name		
Mobile No		
	Will Support the Campaign By	*Tick*
• Volunteering		
• Canvassing		
• Making a donation		
• Phone Campaign		
• Design Support for Posters / Banners		
• Video Creation		
• Audio Editing		
• Collateral preparation		
Additional Information		
You can contribute by : Bank Details / Payment Gateway Details		

Volunteering & Fundraising

Budget Plan:

Below is the rough estimate for a candidate who would like to contest for Assembly election: Election Commission of India (ECI) has increased the expenditure limits for candidates, contesting in Lok Sabha and Legislative assembly polls. The election commission has fixed expenditure limit up to ?95 lakh for the Lok Sabha elections and for the state assembly elections, the expenditure limit is fixed to ?40 lakh .

Activity	Details	Estimated Budget
Nomination Filing: No of Participants: 250	Cost per Person: 120.00 for Lunch	30,000.00
Campaign : Auto	Per Day Auto Rent: 3000 7 Autos Per Day: 7*3000; Total for 15 Days; 15*21000	3,15,000.00
Flex / Mike		50,000.00
LED for campaign	Per Day 12,000 Per Tata Ace ; 2 Tata Ace; 2 * 12,000 = 24,000; Total for 15 Days; 15*24,000	3,60,000.00
Auto Decoration – Fabrication Expense		40,000.00
Candidate Campaign Vehicle	9000 Rs. Per Day; 15 Days * 9000	1,35,000.00
Accommodation for Campaigners + Election Office		4,00,000.00
Food Expense for Campaigners	400 persons, 400 * 200 = 80,000 ; For 15 Days – 15 * 80,000	12,00,000.00
Booth Agent Expense on Election Day & Counting day		2,00,000.00
Stationary Charges for Booth Agents		25,000.00

Print & Social Media Promotions:
   ○ Manifesto Prints / Pamphlets
   ○ SMS push campaign
   ○ Audio Calls
   ○ WhatsApp blast
		12,15,000.00

Total Estimate		**39,70,000.00**

Budget For the Campaign

Make sure to Monitor the cash flow. The campaign will have to constantly monitor how the money is being spent.

<u>Social Media Channels</u>

Leveraging social media channels effectively can greatly enhance your ability to stay connected with people and amplify your outreach efforts during an election campaign. Here are some strategies for each platform:

1. YouTube:

- **Video Content:** Create engaging videos to introduce yourself, share your vision, and discuss local issues.
- **Live Streaming:** Conduct live Q&A sessions, town hall meetings, or virtual rallies to interact directly with constituents.
- **Educational Content:** Share informative videos about your campaign goals, policies, and community initiatives.

2. WhatsApp:

- **Broadcast Lists:** Use broadcast lists to send updates, event invitations, and important campaign announcements directly to supporters.
- **Group Chats:** Create interactive group chats for discussions, feedback collection, and volunteer coordination.
- **Personal Messaging:** Personally engage with voters by responding to queries and addressing individual concerns.

3. Snapchat:

- **Stories:** Utilize Snapchat stories to provide behind-the-scenes glimpses of campaign activities and events.
- **Geo-Targeting:** Use geofilters and location-based targeting to reach Snapchat users in specific localities within your constituency.

4. Facebook:

- **Page and Groups:** Maintain an active Facebook page for official updates and a dedicated group for community discussions.

- **Events:** Create and promote campaign events, town halls, and meet-and-greets to encourage participation.
- **Ads:** Use targeted Facebook ads to reach specific demographics and geographic areas within your constituency.

5. Instagram:

- **Visual Storytelling:** Share compelling photos and videos highlighting your campaign activities, community engagements, and personal stories.
- **Instagram Live:** Host live sessions to interact in real-time, answer questions, and discuss pressing issues.
- **Hashtags:** Use relevant hashtags to increase visibility and reach a broader audience interested in local politics.

6. Twitter:

- **Real-Time Updates:** Tweet frequent updates on campaign activities, events, and policy announcements.
- **Engagement:** Respond promptly to mentions, retweets, and direct messages to foster meaningful interactions.
- **Trending Topics:** Join relevant conversations and use trending hashtags to amplify your campaign messages.

7. Clubhouse:

- **Audio Discussions:** Host rooms on Clubhouse to engage in live audio discussions about local issues, policies, and community concerns.
- **Panel Discussions:** Invite local influencers, experts, and constituents to participate in panel discussions to

broaden perspectives.

- **Networking:** Use Clubhouse's networking features to connect with voters, influencers, and community leaders in real-time.

Tips for Social Media Engagement:

- **Consistency:** Regularly post updates and engage with followers to maintain momentum and visibility.

- **Authenticity:** Share authentic stories and perspectives to build trust and credibility among voters.

- **Feedback Loop:** Encourage feedback, listen to concerns, and demonstrate responsiveness to constituent input.

- **Compliance:** Adhere to social media platform guidelines and electoral regulations to ensure compliance and transparency.

By leveraging these social media channels effectively, you can effectively reach, engage, and mobilize voters, enhancing your campaign's visibility and impact leading up to elections.

Section 3 : Engaging: During the Election /Campaign

CHAPTER TWELVE

Election Process: Nomination to Counting

The Election Commission of India is a permanent and independent body established by the Constitution of India directly to ensure free and fair elections in the country. It is under the jurisdiction of Ministry of Law and Justice, Government of India. At the state level, Election Commission is assisted by the Chief Electoral Officer of the State, who is an IAS officer of Principal Secretary rank. At the district and constituency levels, the District Magistrates (in their capacity as District Election Officers), Electoral Registration Officers and Returning Officers perform election work.

1. •Date for Nominations
2. •Last Date for filing Nominations
3. •Date for scrutiny of nominations
4. •Last date for withdrawal of candidatures
5. •Date of poll
6. •Date of counting

https://www.eci.gov.in/nomination-related-forms

Nomination and Other Forms

Candidate Nomination and Other Forms

1. Form A & Form B - For Lok Sabha, Vidhan Sabha and State Legislative Council elections
2. Form AA & Form BB-For Rajya Sabha and State Legislative Council elections
3. Form-2A-Nomination Paper for Contesting Election to the Lok Sabha (House of the People)
4. Form-2B-Nomination Paper for Contesting Election to the Vidhan Sabha (Legislative Assembly)
5. Form 2C Nomination Paper for Contesting Election to the Rajya Sabha (Council of States)
6. Form-2D-Nomination Paper for Contesting Election to the Vidhan Parishad (Legislative Council) by the Members of the Legislative Assembly
7. Form-2E-Nomination Paper for Contesting Election to the Vidhan Parishad (Legislative Council) from a Council constituency viz, Local Authorities'. Graduates' and Teachers' Constituencies
8. Form 2F-Nomination Paper for Election to the Legislative Assembly of Sikkim from a Constituency

reserved for Sikkimese of Bhutia-Lepcha origin

9. Form 2G- Nomination Paper for Election to the Legislative Assembly of Sikkim from a general Constituency or a constituency Reserved for Scheduled Caste

10. Form 2H- Nomination Paper for Election to the Legislative Assembly of Sikkim from Sangha Constituency

11. Form-5-Notice of withdrawal of candidatures

12. Form-8-Appointment of Election Agent

13. Form-9-Revocation of Appointment of Election Agent

14. Form-10-Appointment of Polling Agent

15. Form-11-Revocation of Appointment of Polling Agent

16. FORM 12D - Letter of intimation to Assistant Returning Officer (for absentee voters)

17. Form-18-Appointment of Counting Agent

18. Form-19-Revocation of Appointment of Counting Agent

19. Form-22A-Appointment of Authorized Agent by Political Parties for election to Rajya Sabha (Council of States)

20. Form-26-Affidavit to be submitted by Candidates along with nomination paper

CHAPTER THIRTEEN

Approvals & Regulations

Organizing an election campaign in India involves obtaining several approvals and adhering to various regulations to ensure compliance with legal and ethical standards. Here are the key approvals and permissions required:

1. Permission for Public Meetings and Rallies:

- **Local Authorities:** Obtain permission from local municipal authorities or district administration for conducting public meetings, rallies, and processions.

- **Police Clearance:** Secure permission from local police authorities to ensure law and order are maintained during the event

2. Use of Public Spaces:

- **Venue Booking:** For events in public spaces or stadiums, book the venue and obtain necessary approvals from the respective governing bodies.

- **Public Grounds:** Get permission from local authorities for using public grounds for rallies and meetings.

3. Traffic Management:

- **Traffic Police:** Coordinate with the traffic police for managing and redirecting traffic during rallies and processions to avoid congestion and ensure safety.

4. Noise Pollution:

- **Sound Permits:** Obtain permits for using loudspeakers and sound systems from local authorities, ensuring compliance with noise pollution regulations, especially during night hours.

5. Campaign Material:

- **Posters and Banners:** Get approval from municipal authorities for putting up posters, banners, and hoardings. Ensure compliance with local laws regarding the placement of campaign materials.

- **Print and Electronic Media:** Seek approval from the Election Commission for any advertisements in print, electronic, and social media to ensure they adhere to the Model Code of Conduct.

6. Financial Regulations:

- **Election Expenditure Monitoring:** Adhere to guidelines set by the Election Commission on election expenditure. Maintain detailed accounts of campaign spending and submit these records for auditing.

- **Bank Account:** Open a dedicated bank account for election expenses, as mandated by the Election Commission, and ensure all transactions are conducted through this account.

7. Campaign Vehicles:

- **Vehicle Permits:** Obtain permits for campaign vehicles from the local transport authorities. Ensure compliance with regulations on the use of vehicles for campaign purposes.

8. Campaign Workers and Volunteers:

- **ID Cards:** Issue identification cards to campaign workers and volunteers to distinguish them from general public and unauthorized individuals.

- **Code of Conduct:** Ensure all campaign personnel adhere to the Model Code of Conduct and other relevant regulations.

9. Election Commission Approvals:

- **Nomination Filing:** Ensure candidates file their nominations with the Returning Officer within the stipulated timeframe.

- **Campaign Schedule:** Submit the campaign schedule to the Election Commission and get approval for campaign events, ensuring they do not clash with any prohibited periods or locations.

10. Digital Campaigning:

- **Social Media Compliance:** Follow guidelines set by the Election Commission for digital campaigning, including approval for social media content and advertisements.

- **Cybersecurity Measures:** Implement measures to ensure cybersecurity and prevent misuse of digital platforms for spreading misinformation or conducting unauthorized activities.

Ensuring compliance with these regulations is crucial for a successful and legally sound election campaign. Engaging with legal and political consultants can also help navigate the complexities of the approval process.

CHAPTER FOURTEEN

Suvidha App

In India, the Election Commission has introduced several technological tools to streamline the process of obtaining approvals and ensuring compliance during election campaigns. One of the primary apps used for this purpose is the Suvidha app.

Suvidha App:

The Suvidha Candidate App is a mobile application developed by the Election Commission of India (ECI) to help candidates with the nomination and permission process during election periods. The app is available on Android platform. To use the Suvidha Candidate App, candidates need to create an account and log in with their credentials. Once logged in, candidates can view the status of their nomination and permission.

The Suvidha Candidate App also provides candidates with a number of other features, including:

- The ability to view the list of permissions required for campaigning.
- The ability to track the status of their permission application.
- The ability to download the permission form and submit it online.

- Track the status of the nomination filed by the candidate.

Here are some of the benefits of using the Suvidha Candidate App:

- It provides candidates with a single platform to track the status of their applications.
- It saves candidates time and provides correct information.
- It helps to promote transparency and accountability in the election process.

Key Features of the Suvidha App:

- **Permission Management:**

  - Candidates and political parties can apply for permissions for rallies, public meetings, processions, and use of loudspeakers.
  - Users can track the status of their applications in real-time.

- **Single Window System:**

  - Provides a single platform for multiple types of approvals required during election campaigns.
  - Ensures a unified and streamlined process for obtaining necessary permissions.

- **Online Submission:**

- Facilitates online submission of applications, reducing the need for physical visits to government offices.
- Digital documentation and uploads ensure a smoother application process

- **Time-bound Approvals:**

  - The system is designed to ensure time-bound processing and approval of applications.
  - Helps in planning and organizing campaign activities without unnecessary delays

- **Transparency:**

  - Provides transparency in the approval process, with clear records of applications submitted, approvals granted, and rejections with reasons.

- **User-friendly Interface:**

  - Easy-to-use interface for candidates, political parties, and election officials.
  - Mobile-friendly application allows for approvals on-the-go.

How to Use the Suvidha App:

- **Registration:**

  - Candidates or authorized representatives need to register on the Suvidha portal or app with relevant details.

- **Application Submission:**

  - Log in to the Suvidha app. Select the type of permission required (e.g., public meeting, rally, loudspeaker use).
  - Fill in the necessary details and submit the application online.

- **Tracking and Updates:**

  - Track the status of submitted applications through the app.
  - Receive notifications and updates on the approval status.

- **Approval and Documentation:**

  - Once approved, download the permission document from the app.
  - Carry the approval document during the campaign events to show compliance with regulations.

cVIGIL App

The cVIGIL App is an innovative tool developed by the Election Commission of India (ECI) to empower citizens to report violations of the Model Code of Conduct (MCC) and other election-related offenses in real-time during elections. The name "cVIGIL" stands for "Vigilant Citizen." This app aims to ensure free, fair, and transparent elections by enabling proactive citizen participation.

<u>Key Features of the cVIGIL App:</u>

Real-Time Reporting:

- Citizens can report MCC violations, such as vote-buying, distribution of liquor, hate speech, and other electoral malpractices.
- Reports are geo-tagged and time-stamped to provide precise information about the location and timing of the incident

User-Friendly Interface:

- The app is designed to be easy to use, allowing users to quickly capture photos or videos of violations and submit them.

Anonymity:

- Users can choose to report violations anonymously, ensuring their privacy and safety.

Quick Response:

- The app promises a rapid response from the election machinery. Once a complaint is registered, it is sent to the concerned authorities for swift action.
- The app tracks the status of the complaint, and the complainant is notified of the actions taken.

Verification and Action:

- Field units verify the complaint within 100 minutes and take necessary action.
- Verified complaints are addressed immediately, ensuring timely intervention.

Comprehensive Coverage:

- The app can be used across India in all states and union territories during the election period.

CHAPTER SIXTEEN

Hitting the Road: Air & Ground Campaign

<u>Air & Ground Campaign:</u>

Hitting the road is categorized in to Air and Ground campaigns. Air campaign includes: Website, Pamphlets / Flyers, Social Media – Face book, You Tube, Instagram, Club House etc., E-Mails, Online Advertisements, Making Telephone calls to voters, Sending out Whatsapp and SMS to voters mobile. Ground campaign includes: Distribution of flyers, Sign Boards / Stickers, Conducting Roadshows / Events, Door to Door visit to voters house.

There are agencies to carry out the above listed activities. You can tie-up with those agencies to be part of your campaign.

Air War & Ground War Campaigns

The campaign should address the answers to the following questions...

- Who you are?
- Why are you contesting for the election?
- What problems you are going to solve?
- How are you going to solve the problem?
- What would be the timeline you will solve the problem?
- Where do you get funds to solve the problem?
- What are the values you will bring in?'

<u>**Targeting the voters:**</u>

There may be 3 different set of supporters:

- Likely Supporter
- Potential Supporter

- Unlikely to Support

  And, 3 Types of Voters:

- Likely Voter
- Potential Voter
- Non-Voter

Your campaign should have a strategy to convince the Unlikely to supporters and Non-Voter base and also ways to convince the potential supporter and Potential voters. Your campaign also needs to consolidate the Likely supporters and Likely Voters this will enable to Win the elections.

Campaign Impact Chart:

The below table helps you to focus on the activity which is more Impactful in terms of connecting with people. Your campaign should focus more on "High" Impact campaign Activities.

Campaign Activity	Impact
Website	Low
Pamphlets / Flyers (Physical)	High
TV	Medium
Local Newspaper	Medium
Radio	Medium
Social Media : Face Book, You Tube, Instagram	Medium
E-Mails / Posts	Medium
Online	Medium
Advertisements	Medium
Stickers / Sign Boards	Medium
Events / Roadshows	High
Door to Door	High
Telephone	Medium
SMS	Medium
WhatsApp	Medium
Clubs / Associations	High
Religious Places	Medium
Near Bank ATMs	Medium
Bus Stand	Medium
Parks	High
Market Area	Medium

High / Medium / Low - Impact Area for Campaigns

"Train Hard, Turn Up, Run Your Best,
And the Rest will take care of Itself." - Usain Bolt.

CHAPTER SEVENTEEN

Fitness: Body & Mind

Any election takes toll on your Body, Mind and Energy. You need to be well prepared to be fit for Before the campaign and also throughout the campaign. Keeping both the body and mind fit is essential for overall well-being and a healthy lifestyle. Here are some tips to help you achieve that:

- **Regular Exercise:** Incorporate physical activity into your daily routine. Aim for at least 150 minutes of moderate-intensity aerobic exercise or 75 minutes of vigorous-intensity aerobic exercise per week, along with muscle-strengthening activities on two or more days a week. Find activities you enjoy, such as walking, jogging, swimming, yoga, or dancing.

- **Balanced Diet:** Maintain a balanced and nutritious diet that includes a variety of fruits, vegetables, whole grains, lean proteins, and healthy fats. Stay hydrated by drinking plenty of water throughout the day.

- **Adequate Sleep:** Get enough sleep each night. Most adults require 7-9 hours of sleep for optimal functioning. Sleep is crucial for physical and mental recovery and overall health.

- **Stress Management:** Practice stress-reduction techniques like mindfulness, meditation, deep breathing exercises, or yoga. Chronic stress can have negative effects on both the body and mind.

- **Social Interaction:** Maintain social connections and spend time with friends and family. Socializing can boost your mood and mental well-being.

- **Intellectual Stimulation:** Keep your mind active by engaging in activities that challenge your brain, such as puzzles, reading, learning a new skill, or playing strategy games.

- **Limit Screen Time:** While technology can be beneficial, excessive screen time, especially on smartphones or computers, can lead to physical and mental strain. Set boundaries and take regular breaks.

- **Avoid Harmful Substances:** Limit or avoid alcohol, tobacco, and recreational drugs, as they can have detrimental effects on your health.

- **Regular Health Check-ups:** Schedule regular check-ups with your healthcare provider to monitor your physical health and address any concerns.

- **Hobbies and Interests:** Engage in activities that bring you joy and fulfillment. Having hobbies and interests can improve mental well-being and reduce stress.

- **Stay Hydrated:** Drink enough water daily to maintain proper bodily functions and mental clarity.

- **Laugh and Have Fun:** Laughter is a natural stress-reliever and can improve mood and mental health. Spend time doing activities that make you happy.

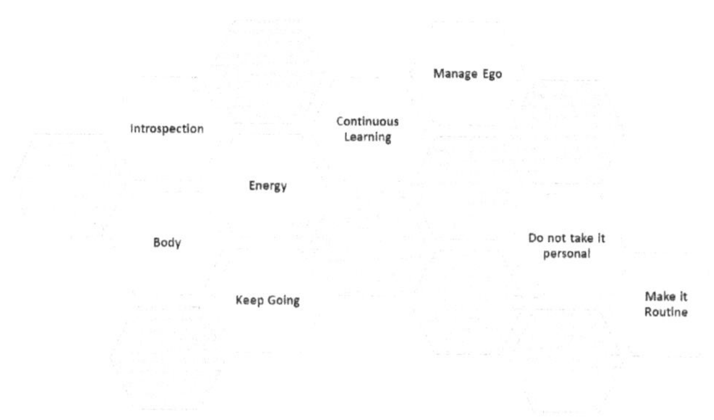

Remember, maintaining a fit body and mind is an ongoing process. Small, consistent changes in your daily routine can make a significant difference over time. Listen to your body and mind, and prioritize self-care to lead a healthier and happier life. An individual who wants to pursue politics as a career must have a very strong body and mind. It's a lengthy career and there is no retirement. To keep it simple, sharing very few significant perspectives that need to be managed.

Though there are several different perspectives, the Mind is the very higher dimension that plays a very crucial role in shaping an individual. One must understand the importance of the mind and its role in everyday life. Mind keeps an individual a happy, strong, healthy, and energetic person.

Knowledge about how the mind works is the very first step and developing complete awareness of how the mind influences everything in and around the person is the second step. It becomes possible to be happy and strong through these two steps. However, it is important the role of all the other factors and their influence on the mind to make it a little easier to become happy and strong. That means maintaining a healthy body, the right food, the right attitude, the aligned people around, and the right habits.

There are several methods like Yoga, GYM, Brisk walking, Games, Meditation, and etc. but that is not important, the important thing is that one have their own routine and develop determination to do it continuously. The chances of starting practice and giving up things are very high, so one must be aware of this drift and have plans to regain the momentum. Probably one can rely on motivational speeches until they become self-motivated and believe in what they do. Simply – Develop an attitude of "**Ensure you do it daily**". It's a journey and continuous process, not something a one-time activity. Must be practiced throughout life. Plan and allocate time for yourself, fix the time slot, never compromise, and become uncomfortable if you do not do it are some of them might help a person to sustain the practice.

Observe the change in body and mind helping your belief system to get stronger. Start observing yourself on your energy levels, how much can you achieve, how

have you performed, an introspection helps anyone to continuously evolve and fine tune.

A person in political career tend to face situations that are disturbing, conflicting conversations, unexpected results ultimately draining the bodily energy very quickly. Identifying and practicing suitable methods will have a long term and positive impact on healthy body and mind.

Conclusion : Stay Connected

Convince people and you win their minds.
Inspire people and you will win their hearts - Ron
Kaufman

Human beings are nothing but emotional creatures. We love, we hate, we laugh, and we cry. The ability to create and nurture genuine connections is not based on how well you speak, what your status is, but merely by your ability to open your hearts to the people. When you open your hearts to people, people will realize that you are in fact REAL and have nothing to hide. People will realize that you actually genuinely care about them, and when they know that, they'll open their hearts to you in return.

Winning hearts and minds in any context, including during an election campaign, involves both emotional connection and logical persuasion. Here's how you can effectively combine these elements to communicate your message:

Emotional Connection:

- **Personal Storytelling:** Share personal anecdotes or stories that resonate with voters and illustrate your commitment to their concerns and aspirations.

- **Empathy and Understanding:** Demonstrate genuine empathy for the challenges faced by constituents, showing that you understand their needs and priorities.

- **Shared Values:** Highlight shared values and beliefs that align with the community's ideals, fostering a sense of unity and common purpose.

Logical Persuasion:

- **Clear Positioning:** Clearly articulate your stance on key issues, backed by a well-defined platform and policy agenda.

- **Evidence-Based Argumentation:**

  - **Data and Research:** Present factual data, statistics, and research findings to support your arguments and proposals.
  - **Expert Opinions:** Reference endorsements or opinions from subject matter experts and respected authorities in relevant fields.
  - **Analysis:** Provide logical analysis of how your proposed policies or actions will benefit the community, addressing practical concerns and challenges.

Constructing Your Message:

- **Identify Common Ground:** Start by framing your message around a situation or problem that everyone can agree needs addressing.

- **Present Solutions:** Offer concrete solutions and initiatives that address identified issues, demonstrating feasibility and practicality.

- **Engage with Transparency:** Be transparent about your intentions, plans, and the expected outcomes of your proposals.

<u>Effective Communication Strategies:</u>

- **Clarity and Simplicity:** Ensure your message is clear, concise, and easy to understand, avoiding jargon or complex language.

- **Visual Aids:** Use visual aids such as infographics, charts, and diagrams to enhance understanding and reinforce key points.

- **Engagement and Interaction:** Encourage dialogue and feedback from voters, fostering a participatory approach to decision-making.

By combining emotional connection with logical persuasion, you can effectively engage voters, build trust, and inspire support for your candidacy. Whether through personal stories that resonate on an emotional level or evidence-backed arguments that appeal to reason, a balanced approach will strengthen your ability to connect with people and win their hearts and minds during your election campaign.

Stay Connected with People from today!
You too can become people's representative!